Copyright © 1987 Nord-Süd Verlag, Mönchaltorf, Switzerland
First published in Switzerland under the title Kamillas weiter Weg
English text copyright © 1987 Rosemary Lanning
Copyright English language edition under the imprint
North-South Books © 1987 Rada Matija AG, Staefa, Switzerland

First published in the United States, Great Britain, Canada,
Australia and New Zealand in 1987 by North-South Books, an
imprint of Rada Matija AG.

Distributed in the United States by
Henry Holt and Company, Inc., 521 Fifth Avenue,
New York, New York 10175.
Library of Congress Catalog Card Number: 86-42943.

ISBN 0-8050-0280-4

Distributed in Great Britain by
Blackie and Son Ltd, 7 Leicester Place,
London WC2H 7BP.
British Library Cataloguing in Publication Data.

Moers, Hermann
    Camomile heads for home.
    I. Title II. Pfister, Marcus
    III. Kamillas weiter Weg. *English*
    833'.914 [J]   PZ7

ISBN 0-200-72900-4

Distributed in Canada by
Douglas & McIntyre Ltd., Toronto.
Canadian Cataloguing in Publication Data available in
Marc Record from National Library of Canada.
ISBN 0 88894 785 2

Distributed in Australia and New Zealand by
Buttercup Books Pty. Ltd., Melbourne.
ISBN 0 949447 37 2

Printed in Germany

Hermann Moers

Camomile

Heads for Home

Illustrated by Marcus Pfister

Translated by Rosemary Lanning

North-South Books

New York   London   Toronto   Melbourne

One day on a farm a little calf was born. She was so small and weak that she couldn't even drink her milk. She could easily have died!

But Joanna, the farmer's daughter, took pity on the little calf. She fed her camomile tea in a baby's bottle, and because the calf loved the tea so much she named her Camomile. When Camomile had sucked the bottle dry Joanna stroked her and told her stories. Day by day, Camomile grew stronger and soon she was able to stand up and drink her milk.

One morning the farmer loaded all the calves into a truck to take them to the market in the town. He even took Camomile. "I won't get much for her," he grumbled. "She's just skin and bones."

"You brute!" mooed Camomile. "Can't you see I'm more beautiful than all the others? I'll win first prize and they'll lead me into a flowery meadow, where there will be a fountain running – full of camomile tea!" And all during the journey to town, Camomile licked her coat with her rough tongue to make it shine beautifully.

In the big market shed there were hundreds and hundreds of calves waiting to be sold. They were all big and strong. No one could see Camomile amongst all the other calves and she was the only one that wasn't sold. Even the farmer forgot all about her and left her behind when he went home.

Camomile stood all alone in the big shed. At first she felt like crying, but then she trotted out through the huge doors.
"I'll show them all who's the most beautiful!" she said to herself, and bravely started to walk home.

On the way Camomile came to a river. It was broad and deep. She looked at her reflection in the water and said, "I'm big and strong. I can leap across in one go." She took a run at the water and jumped. *Splash!* She fell in. "Oh help!" she cried in horror, "I'll never get out again!"

But she didn't want to drown, so she trod water as hard as she could, and with a struggle reached the opposite bank.

"Moo-oo-ooh!" she shouted. "I can swim! See how strong I am!" She sprang into the air with all four legs, as calves always do when they feel like jumping for joy.

Feeling much happier, Camomile walked on until she came to a village. She stopped in front of a greengrocer's shop, her mouth watering. Before anyone could stop her, she gobbled some tomatoes, a cabbage, some apples, a lettuce and some parsley. The shopkeeper rushed furiously out of the shop, put his hands on his hips and asked grimly, "Did you enjoy that?"

Then he looked cautiously to left and right. No one was watching. He quickly put a halter round Camomile's neck and dragged her into his delivery van. Then he drove to the next village and sold her to a farmer.

The farmer took Camomile to join his other calves. "Eat well and fatten yourself up," he said and gave her a pat. Camomile looked around her. There were fences everywhere! Sadly she hung her head — now she couldn't possibly continue her journey home. But soon she was playing with the other calves, happy to be among her own kind.

One hot summer's day, black clouds rolled across the sky.
The farmer hastily drove all the calves into the barn. Almost
at once a streak of lightning flashed from the thickest cloud and
set fire to the barn! The farmer's wife was crying and the farmer
was shouting as they both ran to fetch water. Soon the barn was
burning too. The calves mooed with fear and stamped their feet.
Luckily the fire brigade arrived just in time and drove the calves
and all the other cattle out of their stalls.

Camomile saw her chance to escape and ran! The tip of her tail
had been slightly singed by the fire, but what did that matter
now that she was once again on her way home?

A few days later she came to a town. Camomile couldn't understand why everyone was shouting at her. People were running into shops and doorways. Cars were hooting and swerving wildly. Then a truck stopped beside Camomile. Two men let down the tailgate, grabbed Camomile by the head and tail, dragged her into the truck and drove away to the home for stray animals.

Camomile was put in a stall. She could stretch her head out over
the door and see all the cages full of animals waiting for someone
to come and take them home. Camomile kept nudging
all the keepers and visitors with her pink nose. She wanted to tell
them that she could find her own way home if
only they would let her go. But no one under-
stood what she meant.

"Don't be so sad," said Oswald, the dog in
the next cage. "Someone's bound to want a
beautiful, healthy calf like you sooner or later.
It's just me they don't want. They say I'm ugly
with my bristly eyebrows and whiskery nose.
They don't realise I could be useful to them and
chase away lots of rats."

Camomile beamed with pleasure because
this was the first time someone had called her
a beautiful, healthy calf. But it was true. She
had grown fit and strong on her long journey.

"You'd be just the dog for my farmer," she
said. "There are lots of rats on his farm."

The next time the big gate of the animal home was opened, Camomile unfastened the bolt of Oswald's cage with her nose. Oswald leapt out and opened the door of Camomile's stall and they both ran for freedom.

When Camomile arrived at the farm with her friend Oswald, Joanna recognised her at once. "That's our Camomile!" she cried, clapping her hands with joy. "She's come all the way back to us on her own!" And turning to her father she said seriously, "You couldn't ever give her away again after this!"

"I wouldn't dream of it," laughed the farmer. "And such a big, healthy calf is bound to grow into a beautiful cow." Then the farmer noticed Oswald. "What's that scruffy dog doing here?" he said. He was going to kick Oswald out of the farmyard, but the dog quickly took refuge between Camomile's front legs. Together they stepped back a few paces.

"Look, Camomile and the dog are friends!" cried Joanna. "He must have looked after her on her way home. Anyway, we've been needing a dog for a long time!"

So Oswald was allowed to stay on the farm. Of course,
he slept beside Camomile in the barn. And sometimes,
in the evenings, Joanna told them both a lovely story.